Contents

*S = silver; G = gold; P = platinum; ( ) = the line must be played but cannot be assessed for a Medal.

Levels in bold type indicate that the piece is for mixed saxophones. In each of these cases, the instrumentation is given at the start of the piece. Every other piece can be played either on E flat saxophones or on B flat saxophones.

Sun Seeker

Karen Street

AB 3141

Let My People Go

Spiritual arr. Sarah Watts

AB 3141

3

in memoriam C. B. Z.

Elegy

Jonathan Leathwood

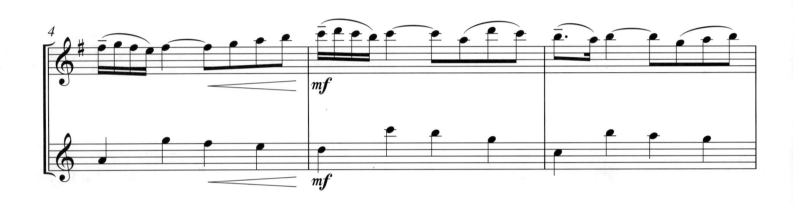

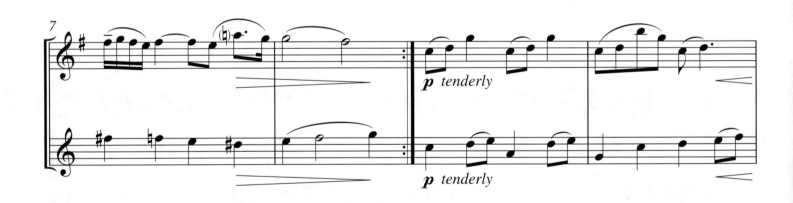

AB 3141

Bull's-Eye Rag

Andy Hampton

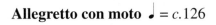

AB 3141

Tango for Two

Jeffery Wilson

Moderato con moto ♩ = *c.*124

AB 3141

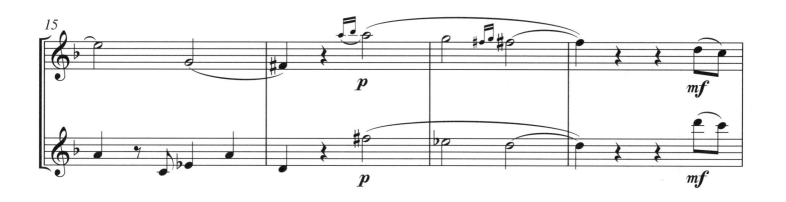

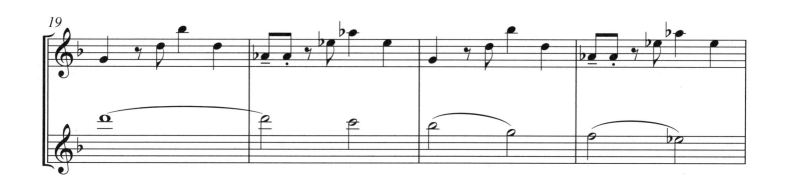

The Oak and the Ash

Trad. English *arr.* Nicholas Hare

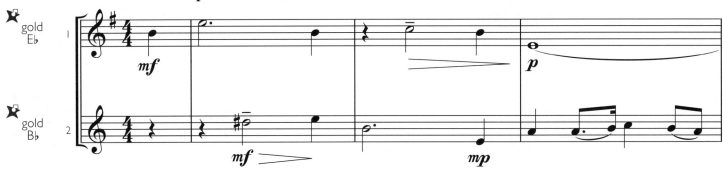

AB 3141

Baroque-n Heart

Cecilia McDowall

Most Irregular!

Paul Harris

Blowing the Blues

Karen Street

AB 3141

Strange World

Nicholas Hare

AB 3141

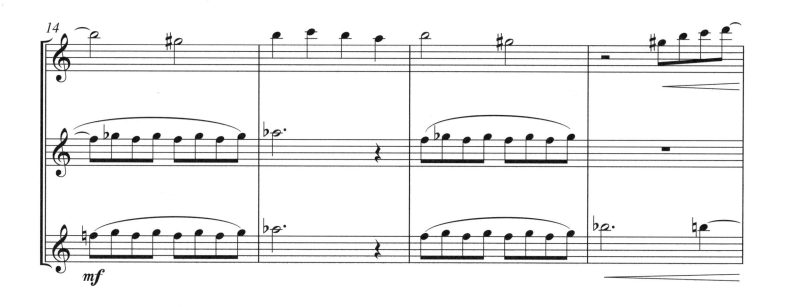

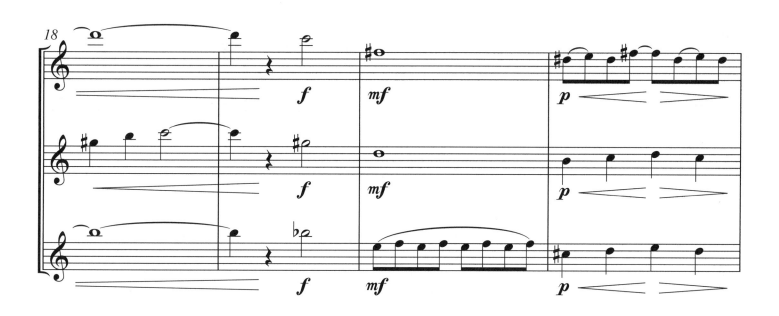

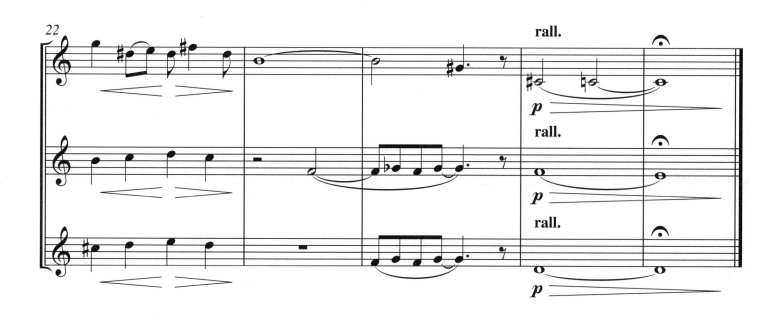

Microvariations
on a motif from Hans Krása's *Brundibár*

Jonathan Leathwood

AB 3141

Gavotte

from French Suite No. 5, BWV 816

J. S. **Bach** arr. Gordon Lewin

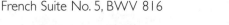

AB 3141

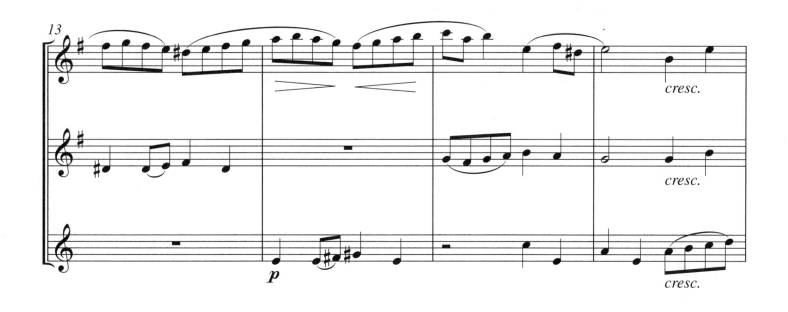

Spanish Bull with Curly Tail

Colin Cowles

Ceremonial Fanfare

Nicholas Hare

AB 3141

Scaling the Mountain

Robert Tucker

AB 3141

Four on Four

Jeffery Wilson

AB 3141

Tienes mi corázon

Trad. Spanish arr. Gordon Lewin

The title means 'My heart is yours'.

Valse triste

Martin Ellerby

AB 3141

A Flavour of Ischia

Paul Harris

AB 3141

The Storyteller

Mark Lockheart

AB 3141

Music Medals Saxophone Ensemble Pieces are five volumes of enjoyable and accessible repertoire for the developing ensemble. Progressively graded – Copper, Bronze, Silver, Gold and Platinum – they contain original pieces and imaginative arrangements for duets, trios and quartets. Covering a wide variety of styles, the volumes provide excellent material for mixed-ability groups as well as being an exciting resource for the individual musician.

- Fun pieces and arrangements in various styles

- Ideal group-teaching material for the developing ensemble

- Five progressively graded volumes

- All pieces selected for ABRSM's Music Medals

ABRSM's Music Medals are assessments that motivate and reward the achievement of group-taught musicians from the earliest stages of learning an instrument. There are five Medals, each covering three activities: playing with others, playing a solo and musicianship options. The pieces in this volume are included in the Music Medals ensemble repertoire lists.

For further information please visit the Music Medals website at www.abrsm.org/musicmedals

Published by ABRSM Publishing, a wholly owned subsidiary of ABRSM

Oxford University Press is the sole worldwide sales agent and distributor for ABRSM Publishing

ABRSM
24 Portland Place
London W1B 1LU
United Kingdom

www.abrsm.org

ISBN 978-1-86096-610-1

9 781860 966101